Other Books by Alexandra Holzer:

Lady Ambrosia: Secret Past Revealed

Growing Up Haunted: A Ghostly Memoir

The End Is Near

Alexandra Holzer

First Edition:
First printing

Cover art by Danielle Gargiulo.

PUBLISHED BY HAUNTED ROAD MEDIA, LLC
www.hauntedroadmedia.com

Cleveland, Ohio
United States of America

One

Ordinary days exist for many, but extraordinary days can coexist for many as well. This day is no different than any other day and starts out well for John. He awakens from the sound of his alarm clock and feels a bit groggy. He feels as if he had drunk a whole bottle of wine the night before. The only problem is he does not drink. He does not smoke or even take over the counter medicines. He believes in the holistic approach. However, on this day he really could use something, anything to take the edge off so he can go to work. Not understanding why he feels this way, he gets up and takes his shower.

What normally takes him twenty minutes to complete feels more like an eternity. Key in the ignition and off he goes to his place of business. Work has been good to him over the years, and he is very lucky in the financial area. As the light is changing, he is getting a surge throughout his body that feels like something is trying to pull him out of his skin. It is an odd sensation, and John doesn't know what to do. He must drive now.

His hands fly off the steering wheel and are pinned to his sides. His feet lock into place, and the car drives itself through the traffic light and forward. Something or someone has taken control over his soul and his vehicle. He accumulates tiny sweat beads that drip down the side of his apple-colored cheeks. A million thoughts should be running through his mind, but he is without thought at this moment. Even his mind is under siege by unseen forces and all he can do is watch it happen.

Earlier that week, John had witnessed a murder. It was not your typical murder in the sense of the word. Out late with friends for dinner, he was one of the last to leave the restaurant. He was always on the lookout for a Mrs. John, but tired and not having much luck in the love department, he decided to go home. He paid the bill for everyone and headed out the door as he said goodnight and thank you to the *Maître D'*. He passed a narrow unlit alleyway on his way to his car, and something caught his eye. Normally, he would have just kept going and minded his business. However, on this night, he could not resist the urge to stop, back up and take a look-see. There, amidst the darkness, circled a smoky white stream of air around a spot on the damp cement ground. John stood there and waited to see what would happen. Something was waiting for his arrival to put on its show. John's heart beat faster as the seconds grew.

There were people walking opposite side of the street going about their business. They did not even notice John standing there.

John's eyes focused in on the spot on the ground and began to see it was a person. But, why was this person there and were they okay? John wanted to move his foot forward to see what was going on, but his feet were not able to move. He could hear a muffled whimper and sobbing in the distance. Suddenly, out of the smoky filtering air arrived a glowing green line that formed an arm. It grew a hand with six fingers and nails so long they faded into the wall of the building in the alley. A gasp of last human breath was heard and the smoky mist sucked up into a ball and dissipated before John's eyes. Finally, his feet were able to move as if slippery ice formed beneath them. Quickly, he went to the spot where a form of a person was lying. There, as he peered down upon the cold, damp, ground, he saw an imprint of what once was a human being.

The imprint showed a figure sprawled out as if it was pinned to the floor. Black ash was left in its place as John bent down to pass his index finger cautiously through it. An odor surrounded the area of burnt flesh. John did not know what it was and became frightened. Realizing what he just witnessed, he decided to rush to his safe haven of a car and flee home and never look back. That night he lay awake in bed pondering all rational explanations that could explain the incident away.

At 4:06 a.m., he dozed off only to awaken at 6:00 a.m., for work. He felt a bit groggy, as if he had drunk a whole bottle of wine the night before.

The car is veering off the road onto a side road. The rain is coming down hard now. If it hits you in the face, you may get bruised. Seattle can be brutal like that. But it is a beautiful city nonetheless. The car is slowing down and goes right into the sand before the shoreline and stops hard. Sand is pushing up everywhere and the front tires seem to get buried a bit. John, motionless the whole ride, lifts up his arms and swings his legs toward the door. He nervously grabs the door handle and forgets to unlock the lock. Jiggling it for a few seconds, it pops up on its own and he falls down onto the soft, wet, inviting sand. He embraces the sand like a security blanket and falls asleep in front of the left front wheel tire.

The lowering sun reflects on John's tired and aged face. He slowly lifts his eyelids up to look into the orange ball and wonders what had happened. He has lost track of time. Dizzy, his head lowers back on the sand and is trying to wake up. A shadow soon covers his entire being and the air grows cold. John opens his eyes again but this time does not see the sun. There is something blocking its way. He should feel frightened but instead, feels much peace and love around him. Confused, he turns his head and looks up at what is covering him. She is so beautiful. Her hair flows away from her face softly and gently. Her eyes are deep and loving as she bends down to lift John up underneath his arms. He is pulled up and standing looking right into her eyes. Her lips are curled and rose-colored like a flower. She speaks in a whisper and tells John what to do.

"Rise. You need assistance and I will help you," she says.

"What is your name? Who are you? Where are we?" asks a confused John.

"My name is Katrina. Now please let us go."

He nods his head in agreement for he is beginning to feel light headed again. She puts him in her car and buckles him in tight. His head falls heavily back onto the car seat and dozes off again. She is looking into the rearview mirror, smiling as she turns on the ignition. They pull away from the shore as dusk is starting to set. Bright lights wake John as he looks up at restaurant sign. "Big's All Night Diner," it reads.

"Good evening sleepyhead, we have arrived," says Katrina. She helps him out of the car and into the diner. They are seated and start the journey of getting to know one another. John is intrigued by this woman and her incredible loving presence. Can he love this soon? Katrina speaks in such a way that her words become minced at times. Her sentences roll like tumbleweeds one after the other, and she speaks with great intelligence. John listens on intently as she tells of her background and how she ended up in Seattle. She owned a small gift shop at the edge of town and was struggling to keep it going. She had no family to speak of and never was married nor had children. From time to time, her words sound a bit ancient and John flinches a bit in awe of that. It is a rare type of conversation to have with a woman, he feels. It seems wholesome and truthful. The whole time with this woman seems comforting. He wants to know why and asks many questions of her. Katrina happily responds to all of them and with great patience. As they finish their meal, it is time to take John home. Seeing there's not the need to go to the hospital, she asks where does he live and is he ready? John replies and off they go toward his home in the suburbs. Pulling up to his house, Katrina pauses and says she would have figured John to live in a building.

"No, that's not for me. I am waiting for my wife, you see, and figured to make home while I can. Life's too short," replies a tired John as he gets out of the car.

He pops his head through the side window to thank Katrina for all that she has done.

"My pleasure, John. I will have your car towed back to this house tomorrow."

John bends back up to turn away but turns around compelled to say one more thing.

Smiling, he says, "Perhaps you may be the wife to fill my home with?" And with that, he confidently walks into his house to collapse for the night. Katrina smiles and drives away, disappearing into the night.

The next morning, the sound of a tow truck backing into a driveway resounds throughout John's house. He awakens feeling refreshed and anew, ready to start his day again. Something has changed in his life. It seems positive. Looking out the living room bay window, he sees his car being let down onto the driveway. He goes out to greet the tower and thanks him.

The tower tells him not to thank him but the lady who paid extra to get it towed so quickly. John smiles and knows it's going to be a great day. Going back into the house, he grabs a shower and calls into his office. They were wondering where he had been this morning and if he was going to work from home.

"That's a silly question, Ingrid. I had an accident and still am coming in. You know me. Nothing can keep me away from my wonderful employees," says John. "Besides, I missed all of yesterday, Monday being so busy as we are, I will be there shortly."

"But, John, today is Monday. You haven't missed work yet. Are you okay? Was the accident Sunday? You should rest and stay home, if you don't mind me saying."

John pauses on the phone, confused again. "Yes, I meant to say that I was just going to be late. See you soon and thanks again, Ingrid." He hangs up the phone and is more puzzled than ever in his entire 38 years of life. Ingrid is a great assistant, and he did not want to worry her. He just played it off and is chalking this up to a lapse of memory and time. He gets ready to go to the office. The phone rings on his tidy desk, and it is Katrina.

"Yes, I was wondering how to reach you. I never got to thank you for all your help and for the towing. How did you find my number?" asks John.

"You left your wallet in my car, so it was easy. If you aren't busy today let's meet for lunch." He gladly responds yes, and they agree to meet across the street from his place of work.

He watches the clock tick away the minutes as noon approaches. "See you later, Ingrid, gotta go." He tips his hat to her as he slips into the closing elevator door. Ingrid rolls her eyes as if to say how odd her boss is acting today.

Across the way is a little cafe that is known for their coffee and crumb cakes. It is actually called, "Cup of Joe's and Place of Cakes." John anxiously hurries across the street, nearly missing a passing car. He hasn't felt this way since he was a schoolboy back in Oklahoma where he's originally from. Everyone knew everyone in his hometown. It was one of those places where if someone passed wind, you'd hear about it. He sits by the window so he can gaze out for his mystery women. Half past twelve, Katrina shows and is more beautiful than John had remembered her. "Could this be the same person?" he thought to himself.

"Hello John, how are you today?"

"Fine, just fine," he says as he stands up to pull out a chair for her. They sit together and smile for a moment.

"John, do you know why I have wanted to meet you here today?"

"No, does it matter? I am just so thrilled to be seated next to a wonderful person such as yourself and to simply say thank you in person."

"John, there is much to tell you and very little time in which to do it in. I am afraid I have to cut this short. I am needed elsewhere," says Katrina.

And with that, she rises up and rushes out of

the cafe looking for something. She disappears again, and John is left alone to ponder his confusing thoughts which are all over the place like a jigsaw puzzle when you first open the box.

"Coffee sir? Sir, would you like something to drink?" asks the impatient waitress.

"What, oh, I am sorry. My party just left and I wasn't ready. Yes, I will have a cup of Joe and a coffee crumb cake, please."

The waitress leaves and John stares out the window searching for Katrina. He senses something is happening to him and it is not one single thing that he can put his finger on. This bothers him because he is a very rational, conservative man who his whole life has been based on love and family matters that always made sense. This is the first time in his life that something or someone does not make any sense at all. As he finishes up his meal, he pays the check and gets up to leave the cafe.

Suddenly, while outside on the street getting ready to cross, something flashes by him and burns his face a bit. It looked like a white light of some sort, but there was another color, perhaps green. When he returns to his office Ingrid asks if had he been to the beach. After replying no, he asked why.

"You're all sunburned, John. Take lotion next time if you are going to eat at the beach."

John half smiles, goes into his office and closes the door. There, he pulls out a mirror, and much to his horror, sees his face all sunburned.

"It wasn't like that before I left here. What is the deal here?"

A little frustrated, he looks around for some moisturizer and finds none. He decides to call it quits for today as to seeing how he is not able to get any real work done. He tells Ingrid to transfer all calls to his cell and he will be working from home for the rest of the day. He is starting to feel dizzy again and does not want to drive before it gets worse.

On his drive home, normally he does not look around to see what is going on but this time feels the need to. People walking by seem to be changing colors. One man looks paler than the next. One woman looks darker then the next. It is very odd. Dogs being walked seem angry and bark at each other as they pass by. Babies in their carriages are all crying. The sky is always gray in Seattle, but this time it seems more green-gray. A storm is on the horizon, a wicked storm that could knock out your power and blow over trees and people. John does not like this feeling and is certainly not happy about what he is seeing.

At home, there are no messages on his phones and everything seems to be very still and lifeless. It is growing cold now and he gets his favorite gray sweater with moth holes in it. His mother had given it to him before she had passed seven years ago. His father died shortly after her. He always believed that his parents were a pair of lovebirds. When one dies, shortly after so does its mate. Not having any siblings, he has made many friends over time. They are his family now. He is hoping Katrina could be his missing piece if only he could get her to sit again and chat.

Just as that thought crosses his mind, he feels the need to go outside. Out the back patio door, onto the beautiful stone path leading to his well-manicured garden he goes. Rain begins to fall lightly on his head. He walks up to a rose bush he had planted in memory of his parents' passing and peers over it. There, he sees an incredible image that freezes him in time. The raindrops stop dropping and are motionless in the air. John could count how many are in front of him. It's surreal.

There, over the hedge, is a pure white bright formation spinning in place. It creates a whirlwind around itself and the leaves on the grass are stirring about. It turns toward John. As he stares on gazing at its beauty and pureness, he is not afraid. He wants to know what it is and why it is in his garden. A voice bellows out from within this light and calls his name. It then pulls itself into a human form and becomes Katrina.

"No, it can't be," thinks John. "It just can't. Doesn't make sense."

Katrina advances in a gliding motion with her feet not touching the ground beneath her.

"Don't be afraid, John," she whispers, holding out her hand to him. "I didn't mean for you to see me this way. I suppose we are connected and you sensed my being here. You came looking for something. Me."

"But, how? Why?" asks John.

"Come sit with me and I will tell you why I am here," she says as she pulls him over his hedge top and down onto the moist grass. The raindrops are still frozen yet he can pass right through them without disturbing one drop. It is quite magical. Dust particles are floating still in the air. Trees don't move. Sounds are not heard. It is as if they are in a protected bubble and no one nor anything living can see or hear them at this very moment.

Two

"My name is not Katrina. That is my given human earth name. I am Glidiana, Angel Helper to the Gods above and Protector of Life. I have been sent here to seek out a pure soul in order to help unite others against the evil that has begun here in Seattle. It is moving rapidly state-to-state, claiming pure souls and leaving the damned and rotted to roam the earth. When they perish, they will go to the bottom realm into their own darkness. All the good souls will no longer be around to go to the upper realm into the light. Our Kingdom is losing all the good souls and evil will outnumber us all. The earth shall grow dim and lifeless. Only those left will be that of a rotten core walking around in their human bodies without spirit."

John is in shock and does know what to say.

"There's more," Glidiana explains. "This is the mark of the world ending. Jesus will return, and upon his return all remaining will be judged."

"You mean Judgment Day is happening, now?" asks John.

"If you do not help me John, yes."

"Why me? What do I have to do with all this Bible stuff? Jesus Christ, what is going on here?"

Glidiana looks at him sternly and John apologizes for saying the Lord's name in vain.

"John, do you know what your true name means? You are the giver of life and a true soul. You have been chosen by God to help lead the cause to stop the end of the world from happening."

John musters up the strength to ask a question. "You know Jesus, personally?"

"Yes, John, I do, and he is not happy with your kind at this moment. Mankind has been destroying the very fabric of life. All the good that it was intended for has been turned bad. Your kind is unappreciative of what God has given you. If Jesus must return here on earth since his last appearance, then, this world as you know it shall end. The skies will turn red and the earth will shake and rise up to heaven, and all will become one. We have no more time. We must go," explains Glidiana.

She gets up and points John in the direction toward his car.

"We need to find four pure souls and gather at the beach to form a ritual. Here, we can summon the beast before it is too late."

With those last words hanging on to the still air, the raindrops begin to fall and everything around them moves. John is to do what he was told. He now understands his purpose in life, even though he may lose his own life to save others. His reward would be to see his parents again, maybe to even meet Jesus. Without hesitation and more clarity, John gets into his car to find four good souls and bring them to the beach. He doesn't know how he is going to do this but he has to start now. The skies have not cleared up, and the feeling of death and destruction looms overhead. John has been given a third eye and is now connected to this angel. He can sense and see ahead things to come. He will never be the same person as he was before he met Glidiana.

Driving by splashing in the wet streets, he searches for friend number one, Heinrich. Heinrich lives alone in town and works with John as his partner. He is a bit older than John and from Germany. He still has his accent. John is certain he makes a good first start as far as souls go. This man has given most of his life to charity for children and donates all the time. He lost his wife to a rare form of cancer many years ago. He doesn't want to re-marry, so he remains alone and content in doing so. He arrives at the home of Heinrich and finds that he is asleep. He rings his night bell furiously until he sees the upstairs light go on. A sleepy Heinrich answers the door to an anxious John.

"What is it? Are you okay? Come in, man, you look horrible."

"No, no time. Will explain in the car. Please, just come with me now as is," rushes John.

Before Heinrich can respond, he is whisked away into the night with John. On the way to the next home, John feverishly explains what has happened to him and what is happening to the world. Heinrich is in disbelief. He has never heard his business partner and longtime friend speak such things. For fear he has gone over the deep end, he goes along with the plan. He thinks John may commit suicide.

The next home is Eli's. He also works with John and Heinrich but is only an assistant to Heinrich. He is young, untainted and without a mean bone in his young body. He is a perfect specimen for the ritual. He is up, of course, at this late hour, watching a movie and eating. The young have a fabulous metabolism that way. When he answers the door he, too, is whisked away and John explains in the car what is going on. Heinrich gives his version to Eli through facial gestures. Eli is the most confused of them all, but he thinks he has been kidnapped for a night out on the town so he, too, goes along with this plan.

Next on the list as John is feverishly driving about is a women named Lauren. She is Heinrich's cousin whom John has adopted as his own cousin. She, too, is a bit aged but such a love of life. She has grown children who had moved out years ago. She, also, lives alone and had lost her husband only this past year. This one will be a bit of a challenge.

"Heinrich, please, can you go in and make up a story to her so she'll come with us?"

Heinrich grunts and gets up still thinking his friend is going over a cliff. He turns to John and says, "And how, pray tell, am I going to get her in the car? What am I to say to her at this late hour?"

"Just tell her it's an emergency with me and you need help to get me to the hospital. She'll come and the rest we'll deal with while driving. Hurry, we have little time. The sun will rise soon and then it will be too late."

Meanwhile in New York, a reported one hundred thousand people were missing without any trace of bodies to explain the mystery. This was growing in numbers throughout all the states. Only a few places remain untouched of this phenomenon.

Heinrich gets Lauren into the car. Her hair is in rollers with a scarf wrapped around it to hold it in place. She is pushed into the back seat next to Eli.

"Eli can you please move over a bit. I feel squished."

Eli gives Lauren a sideways glance.

"I just wanted to be close to you and those lovely hair worms you've got going there."

The look on Lauren's face could scare away the nastiest of demons as she glares directly at Eli. Turning her head back, she looks out the window trying to remain calm.

"You guys think beauty just comes naturally for us gals, but I've got news for you. It does not!"

Eli begins to try and respond cautiously but can't help himself.

"Clearly that's obvious."

Lauren whips her head back around like *The Exorcist* and rather than spitting up a pea soup like liquid, she lets out a huge noise.

As Eli's about to respond back, Heinrich steps in.

"Would you two just stifle yourselves back there? You're like a bunch of kids and now is not the time!"

Eli and Lauren look down at their feet feeling slightly silly.

"That's more like it! And if either of you kick the back of my seat, it's time out! Got it?!"

Both Eli and Lauren nodded in compliance to Heinrich's request.

Heinrich faces front again, nervously waiting for the next steps in this crazy night. Everyone knew each other, so it was not as awkward. Lauren begins asking a million questions.

"John, what happened? Heinrich wouldn't

say. Are you hurt? Are you bleeding? Which hospital are we going to?"

She didn't even ask why Eli was there. Heinrich rolled his eyes and muttered something under his breath., "Do you see what your insanity is causing? You have gone completely nuts. You answer her. I am done." With a huff and a sigh, he folds his arms and looks out the window. Just then, as sweat is sliding down John's face, he hears Glidiana.

"John, this is your revelation. 'The revelation of Jesus Christ which God gave him to show to his servants what must soon take place; and he made it known by sending his angel to his servant John, who bore witness to the word of God and to the testimony of Jesus Christ, even to all that he saw. Blessed is he who reads aloud the words of the prophecy, and blessed are those who hear, and who keep what is written therein; for the time is near.'"

A bright light shines in John's face as an oncoming car fast on the approach heads directly at them. There's no time to slow down or move over. They are driving on a rocky and curvy highway. Nowhere to turn. As they scream, John's car rises up above the other car and right smack down back onto the highway. It stops short. Everyone looks at each other and asks if anyone is hurt.

"What the tomfoolery just happened?" bellows a very confused Heinrich.

"I know this all seems rather odd, but trust me when I tell you it's only going to get stranger as the night goes on!" replies John.

Heinrich shakes his weary head and looks out to the night sky. As he focuses back on John's flushed face, he tries to make sense of all of it.

"Look, my friend, I've never doubted you, but you've got to realize that this is just too darn weird, even for us!" Heinrich exclaims.

"Well, there was that one time when we were supposed to have that meeting in Ohio. Remember how that all went? The dancing bears, unforeseen snowstorm and a town straight out of a horror movie?"

"Yeah," chuckled Heinrich.

"Don't forget the tumbleweeds! I swear I thought we were in the *Twilight Zone* or something!"

They start the car back up and are heading toward the last house.

"Where to next on this insane night that you lead us on?" asks Heinrich.

"Peter's home," John replies.

"Who's Peter?" asks Heinrich.

"Peter is a long-time friend I have known since I moved here. He was the first person to befriend me. Without him, I don't think I could have survived this place. He was my earth angel."

"Nice but you speak in tongue. Angels. What are you talking about? When we get back from this little excursion, you are having your head examined, my friend. And I will be there when the results come in!" belts out Heinrich.

Ten minutes later they arrive at Peter's home. He still lives with his mother, something John misses.

"This time, I'll go get him," John says and there are no arguments. He pulls into Peter's driveway, gets out of the car, and gently knocks on the door using the door knocker. It is now 4:33 a.m. and very late or very early. It is Peter's mother who answers the door.

"Yes, can I help you?" she asks half awake.

She hasn't realized it is John. It takes a few moments before seeing his face.

"John, my goodness. What brings you here at this ungodly hour?"

"Please, don't say that word. Listen, I don't have much time, so I can't explain, but I do need Peter. Is he here?" asks John.

"Yes, of course but he's sleeping."

"Wake him, please!" shouts John. "Sorry to shout. I am very tired and it's very late. It's an emergency. Please, can you wake him for me?"

With that being said, Peter's mother turns to wake her son. Within seconds, which feels like forever, Peter appears fully awake.

"John, thank God it's you. I have to talk to you," says Peter.

He pulls John to the corner of the room and tells him of the dream he was having. It was of death and destruction and the end of the world nearing.

"The strangest part of the dream was that you were in it, leading the way. And now here you are. How bizarre is that? It felt so real."

John grows pale and hurries Peter along. As John rushes him into the car the rest of the gang grows more impatient.

"What took you so long?" asks Heinrich.

At first John doesn't answer and just gets back on the road. Once they are on their way John turns to Heinrich very flustered.

"Look! I'm doing the best I can and under the circumstances, I, I, well just that I've got this under control!"

As Heinrich looks to the back of the car, then back to John his eyes widen and lips tense up.

"Fine. Fine, fine, fine. You've got this alllllll figured out, yet here we are whizzing around again in the middle of the night!"

John slows down the car, gives Heinrich a

steadfast hearty stare then speeds back up looking towards the road ahead.

"And another thing, I don't believe in all this superstition, but yet, here we are! So, you know I'm just pointing that out, is all," replied a very annoyed Heinrich.

Suddenly there's a sound like tiny pebbles being thrown at the window. As the group peers out into the night they realize that it isn't rocks hitting their windows. It is a swarm of locusts. The sky is filled with them, creating a bumpy effect when looking up. It is horrible.

John belts out, "The fifth angel has blown its trumpet! It's almost time!"

John doesn't know what beach he is supposed to go to. He comes to a stop sign and hears a hissing sound. Serpents slither out from the grates onto the city streets. They turn a reddish-brown tint. John panics and tries to find the right beach. Finally, he comes across one that seems to feel right. He swerves into the sand sideways, almost tipping over the car.

When John was a little boy, he always had a feeling of greatness. He would grow up some day to do great things. In his adult life, he had accomplished a successful publishing business but never felt fulfilled until now. What was about to happen was of great importance and would change mankind. Finding the right wife was no longer a concern. Keeping his and everyone else's life was his goal and calling.

At age 15, John was working the farm and started using the tractor that his father slowly had taught him over the previous two years. This was a proud day for John and his folks. He climbed up the tractor and started it up with ease. He began to plow the soil so his dad could plant corn seeds. All of a sudden, a cat ran across the field, and it was too late for John to notice and stop the tractor. He thought for sure he had killed the poor thing, but, much to his amazement and relief, he turned around and saw that the cat was unharmed. Running about to the other side of the field it had used one of its nine lives.

He chalked it up to simply missing the animal, but his father saw it and said it should have been dead. At age 20, his father had cut his thumb while sawing some wood to make a table for his wife. When John saw the accident and the blood gushing about, he quickly grabbed his father's thumb and wrapped it up in a cloth that was hanging from the fence post. He called out to his mother to get the first aid kit. When John and his father looked down at the wounded finger, it had been healed. John removed the blood-soaked cloth and saw that the thumb was not cut. It was as if divine intervention had played a part that day when John touched his father's finger. John's father always said that he thought his son was gifted with the power to heal. Of course, this was hard to prove and where they lived it did not go over too well. So, as time went on, all the stories were put away and never spoken of again until now.

"Heinrich, we need to get out of the car and wait for her to come" a shivering John says.

"It is 40 degrees and raining. We will all get our death of colds if we do that," huffs Heinrich.

"I don't care, we will get worse if we don't. Everyone, please get out of the car and follow me. There are blankets in the trunk to drape over you if you're cold," explains John.

Winds pick up speed and the water seems angry and thrashes about on the fading shoreline. The moon is full and hidden by the reddening sky. They unsteadily drag through the sand to the middle of the beach. There they stand shivering and so tired they can hardly keep their eyes open. John fears this was all a big mistake and begins to doubt himself. What if this was the wrong place? He is responsible for these people standing before him putting their lives on the line for little to no explanation as to why they're out there in the middle of the night, freezing. "What is to become of this night? Would it ever end?" John wonders as he shakes uncontrollably from fear and the unknown. The cold wind comforts him more than the potential outcome of the evening.

Then, as he closes his eyes, he prays. He prays harder than he has ever prayed in his life.

"We give thanks to thee, Lord God Almighty, who art and who was, that thou hast taken thy great power and begun to reign. The nations raged, but thy wrath came, and the time for the dead to be judged, for rewarding thy servants, the prophets and saints, and those who fear thy name, both small and great, and for destroying the destroyers of the earth. Amen."

The heavens open up and the Ark of the Covenant shows through. The sky fills with lighting, voices, thunder, hail and now the earthquake begins. The ground beneath everyone shakes vigorously without warning. A voice breaks through the winds and speaks biblical messages to the group. A bright white light slowly forms around them just above their heads.

"Behold before you, it is I, Glidiana that speaks. John, you have done well and the time has come to summon the beast. I warn you this will not be an easy task. The earth has begun to crack and crumble and your inner peace is needed now the most. Pray for life and pray for the souls who were taken by evil and return them to the Kingdom where they belong."

And with that, the light fades and so does the voice. Everyone is speechless except Heinrich.

"Well, now that's an entrance if I ever saw one. Okay, I believe. I believe we are ALL crazy! Now what, brother John?

Three

In Chicago, news had spread of the disappearances of people from around the globe. It was soon becoming a phenomenon. All the prisons remained filled and not one prisoner anywhere in the world was affected. It seems to be only the good are vanishing. There had been sightings of a cloud-like formation hovering over something and then disappearing into the air. An odor preceded it that smelled of fire or burnt wood. Some said it is that of rotting flesh. One by one, peoples' judgments were revealed.

Rome is quickly on its way to being another city with loss of good life. Considering that the

Vatican City is a center target against many evils, it is here where much destruction can occur. The priests lay awake at night praying as they hold their crucifixes tightly in one hand while holding holy water in the other. It is making its move across the world, no crucifix or holy water can change the path of its destruction. It knows where it wants to hit as the chanting of prayers deafen the night sky. People flee to churches everywhere. Chaos and pandemonium set in. This, of course, is part of the plan from the unknown happening right now. It knows where the people feel most safe, and in that safety is where they are most vulnerable. Rome is not the place to be, yet many flock there feeling and thinking quite the opposite. People flee to churches everywhere. Chaos and pandemonium set in.

"It has begun Lord. It has begun" whispers John.

He slowly seems to slip into a trance-like state. His friends watch helplessly.

"Then, I saw another beast which rose out of the earth; it had two horns like a lamb and it spoke like a dragon. It exercises all the authority of the first beats in its presence, and makes the earth and its inhabitants worship the first beast, whose mortal wound was healed," John says in a deep and steady voice.

Heinrich does not like the sound of his friend's tone nor does he trust what John is saying.

"Quickly, we're here for a reason. Let's put our heads together and see what we can do to help the angel and John."

Lauren was so tired that she sits down even with the earth moving. Peter and Eli review the night's events and try to piece together what it is they are all supposed to do. One comes up with the idea to draw their names out in the sand and see if there is any hidden biblical meaning to it with a message. So, Eli finds a stick and begins to write the names in the order John picked them up. Heinrich, Eli, Lauren, Peter. Meanwhile, John starts spewing out phrases.

"For men have shed the blood of saints and prophets, and thou hast given them blood to drink. It is their due!" screams John.

The others are now frightened of what they see. Eli is feverishly trying to find some meaning in their names. Then a huge gust of wind blows past and removes most of the letters spelled out in the sand. They are left with, He, El, L, P. Just then, Glidiana returns from heaven and in her possession she holds a key and a chain.

"With this great chain and key, you must bound the devil to the bottom of the earth's crust where no light may enter. There, you will lock the chain with this key. Salvation shall be yours and your earth shall be free. Jesus is nearing. Please, hurry quickly and awake John. He has seen enough." And with that, she floats back up to heaven.

"John, wake up. John, we have orders from the angel you see. Please, wake up," says Heinrich who is shaking his best friend out of a trance.

John wakes up and looks around, confused about what just happened.

"Is it over?" he asks.

"No, my friend, it hasn't even begun yet. But we are all here for you and have been shown the way" says Heinrich.

They explain to John what Glidiana said and show him the great chain and key. Just then, the sea bubbles over and there are hundreds of dead fish strewn about. Everyone backs away toward the car.

Back in Rome, the Vatican was in an uproar over the controversy of the world coming to an end, but they could not explain all the missing people. Some said it was aliens while others said they saw the hand of the devil take them. No one knew what to believe. Cities were in lockdown formation. People weren't allowed to enter or leave.

In one of the priest's chambers was a priest praying heavily and sobbing for mankind. A green like mist slid underneath the door and moved right up behind the priest. Others were in the hall passing by his room when, suddenly, they heard a gurgling noise then a thud as if something fell to the floor. The men in the hall rushed over to the door, and when they entered the room they found nothing. There was burnt ash in a circle on the floor. Then the odor came.

"Tell the Pope, tell him it has begun here. We need orders as to what to do with this demon," commanded the high priest to the others.

They rushed down the hall to find their Holy Father. An exorcism would be needed and only his Excellency and the council could authorize it. They needed to find just cause and proof that a demon existed within the Vatican. The last time this ritual was performed was several decades past. Inside the council's hearts, no one was certain if they could cast out the demon that Satan has sent to end the world. This would be an exorcism like no other in the entire history of casting out demons.

Meanwhile, back in Seattle, John has a vision of the Vatican and what they are planning to do. John begins to shake his head side-to-side in disagreement.

"No, no, no, don't disturb the beast. He will not come here then. Let him to me," cries out John as if he was experiencing some sort of pain.

The others look at him, not knowing what to make of their friend's statement. Turning to Heinrich, John tells him that they are in great danger and need to contact the Vatican right away.

"Oh sure, that should be a breeze. Why not? I suppose it's possible considering the night we are all having," remarks Heinrich.

John is not amused.

"We need to begin the ritual now," yells out John with his arms spread out as if to fly.

"You are really losing your nutty marbles! We've come all this way, and you're still talking like you're some kind of super human being that's going to soar up into the sky and fix it all! That's not how life works, John!"

John puts his arms down, lifts up his tired head and looks at the group.

"Guys, I get it. Really, I do. Look where we are. Do you not see what is happening? This is not a movie plot. It's real life. I need you all to trust me, please. Even if it gets ugly."

Eli looks around as everyone is focused on the sky. He gulps hard and points upwards towards the night.

"Ahhh, guys? What the heck …"

He's as white as a ghost. Here it comes!

Battling the strong gusts of wind that are trying to take away his words, John tells everyone to form a circle and hold hands.

"Whatever you do, don't let go," warns John.

He places the great chain, creating a circle-like circumference and seals it in place. He takes the key and places it in his pocket. The trap is set.

At this very moment the Pope has begun to prepare his council for the exorcism. All the priests gather in the incense smoked-filled room. Three priests wearing tall black odd-shaped hats carry Roman symbols on the front. They begin to walk around in a circular motion. Each priest has a long chain with a ball that holds the burning incense. They swing the chain side-to-side as they are getting ready to be seated. In the back of the immense room, is the Pope looking on for guidance and prayer. He sits with the Holy Bible on his lap and holding a crucifix in his left hand. His eyes are closed as he chants a prayer of protection. The circle is to be sealed with the chant for protection before they can summon the demon. Suddenly, the room lights begin to flicker off and on like a broken all-night neon sign. They are not alone.

The demon that Glidiana refers to as "the beast" has been purposely waiting in the dark for this to happen.

Something is not right, and John senses this. Back at the beach, John is about to speak the necessary incantation to begin the process when suddenly, the Arch Angel Gabriel appears from the stormy sky face down in front of John.

"Halt! You must not utter a single word," commands Gabriel. "They have already begun theirs and the beast knows. It will never come here now. You must go to it."

"I do not understand. I was told it is to be this way, here and now. Why is it changing, and how am I supposed to get to Rome?" asks John.

John begins to cry out as if in writhing pain again, and suddenly the circle is broken. The great chain is left in the sand and Gabriel grabs John underneath his arms. Together they soar into the stormy red clouds and vanish into the chaotic night. Heinrich and the others look on in utter amazement.

"Wow! Now that's what I call spectacular. Did you see his wings? Much bigger than that other gal, what was her name? Oh yes, Glidiana," observes Heinrich.

Lauren speaks up to her mouthy cousin.

"Just shut up! Can you not see what has just happened? John is gone. He is being taken to Rome and without any of us for backup. The plan has been altered and I fear he is in grave danger more now than ever. We must pray for him."

Having said that, everyone bows down his or her heads and prays for John's safe return home. They pray for the world and all its departed good souls to be returned to the Kingdom of God.

Four

"It's very brisk up here. And I cannot see a thing in front of me. How tall are you by the way?" asks a nervous and typically chatty John.

"Remain calm. Hold on to my belly feathers for they shall warm you. There is nothing to see for life as you once knew it is no longer in existence. When the time nears, you will see what needs to be seen. I am as tall as you see me to be," explains Gabriel.

"Okay. Thank you, sir," John answers.

"Ha," bellows out Gabriel. "You are certainly one of the funnier ones I must say. I am not a sir. Gabriel will do just fine. John, there is much work to do still and we approach Rome."

Gabriel begins to slow their descent.

Now, shouting through the rough and noisy winds Gabriel braces John.

"Place your head down as we are to land shortly!"

John does as he is told. Gabriel's warm body makes John feel safe and secure in a time where that does not exist anymore. He does not want to let go.

"Gabriel, take me with you. I will go to your Kingdom. I do not want to go down there. Please, let me stay in your world," John pleads.

There is no reply. They are making their descent in a swooping motion downward, landing harshly onto the stone ground in back of the Vatican. There isn't a soul around in the physical sense of the word. Everything is dark, and only the sliver of the moon that has changed its color to red shines through onto the wet stone paved ground. It is the eye of the storm. The smell of rotting flesh and burning wood infiltrate the air. John is left standing looking around to what comes next.

Inside the Vatican, the three priests have sat down in their chairs that are surrounding the circle they have formed. Each one has his Bible open to the same passage. Rose petals are strewn everywhere to signify peace and love. White candles light the room and the air is heavily perfumed with incense burning. Smoke lingers thickly in air and stays motionless in place over the circle. A creaking noise is heard from somewhere in the room. There, in a dark corner where light cannot reach, awaits the opportunity to pounce and finish the job.

Until now, the Pope has been heavily guarded and protected. He is a prime soul that will be a nice prize for Satan. This soul he will hang on display in the underworld as a trophy of his victory. The Pope is vulnerable as he is aged twenty years since this has all begun. One of the prophecies was that at the start of the end, the Pope will grow white quickly and his skin will show signs of death looming. When this happens, the earth shall meet the bottomless pit and Jesus will come to begin the end.

Around the world, all the cities have grown quiet. What once use to be bustling places to work and dwell are now modern-day ghost towns. Those who remain are the spiritless souls who seek out harm and destruction. Crimes are being committed everywhere, and Jesus has begun his descent to earth.

Heinrich and the others stop in the middle of their prayers and notice the sea is changing. The water has stopped bubbling and the winds are dying down to a calm roar.

"Is it over? Is it done?" questions Heinrich, opening his eyes as he looks around.

He closes his eyes again and takes in a deep breath. Since his wife's passing, he has been unable to feel deeply. He reaches deep down into his core and tries to feel what is happening. He is shown something—a tormented image that is yet to come. He opens his eyes and looks to Eli.

"No, we are in the eye of the storm. Quickly, we must leave and find shelter elsewhere from here. Back to the car, now!" Heinrich says hurriedly.

Tiredly but swiftly, the group runs back to the car lying in a ditch of sand. Eli starts the car but cannot back it up. The wheels are spinning in the front.

"Oh, God, please help," says Eli. He starts the car again, and he spins the car deeper into the sand.

Everyone is now praying. Suddenly, the car reverses out of the sand by unseen forces and spins around at a 180-degree angle, then revs up and stops. Eli and Heinrich look at each other smiling, then look out ahead of them and forward they go driving as fast as they can. They head toward John's home. It is chosen to be the place to go in hopes they will see their friend there.

Back in Rome, Gabriel speaks one last time to John. "Listen very closely John. Inside this building the beast awaits you. He thinks he has won with his trickery. You must clear all your thoughts and leave any doubts you've ever had here with me. This will keep you out of harm's way. He knows you are here and grows more anxious. John, it is all up to you to go in and fight the beast. Do not let it get near the Pope. Draw it to the circle. There, you will find salvation."

With that having been said, Gabriel lifts up off the ground and away from John into the red sky. For the first time, he is alone since this all began. He has a flashback. At age 30, he had begun his business. The night before he was to meet with his potential partner, Heinrich, he had a dream. At the time, it seemed ridiculous and even absurd to believe it was anything to worry about. Now, it may have been a premonition of the future. John wasn't listening then. He was too closed-minded to even fathom that one could see the future and be accurate. He believed in a higher being, but he never felt comfortable in discussions about the afterlife and psychic phenomenon. He always sat unusually quiet.

"Why didn't anyone tell me sooner?" asks John looking out into the night.

"Why throw this on me now? I could have prepared. We could have won already!" shouts an angered John.

"Hush!" comes a voice out of nowhere.

"You would not have been ready. Time means nothing. You cannot prepare for the coming of Jesus. You carry all the necessary tools needed to defeat the beast. Clear your thoughts, John. You have been warned."

The voice trails off in the distance. The voice, unrecognizable to John, silences him. Looking up, John notices there aren't any lights on in any of the visible rooms in the Vatican. He takes that as a sign. Rome is the last place to be hit with the phenomena of people vanishing without a trace. He walks around to the front of the grand building. There are no guards or persons at the front. It's easy to simply open the large heavy doors and walk in. As he enters the holy grounds of the Vatican, a surmountable energy surgesthroughout his entire being. The ceiling reaches up to the heavens. Gold-lined walls and ancient artwork hung everywhere. This was the first time John has never visited anyplace outside his hometown. Seattle was the first and would be content on being the last. John is not much for traveling and is happy to stay put. Traveling by angel, though, was certainly a first.

"If I ever get out of this alive, I hope to have one more trip with an angel," John mutters as he moves about the grand entranceway.

Looking up and down and all around his environment, he forgets for a moment what has happened. He feels as if he is the only human being in the world and is king for the day to be alone in this place of historical presence. It is an overwhelming sensation. For a simple, hometown boy like John, this is a thrill and a half. He shakes his head and wakes up from his dreamlike state and peers down the hall. He smells something burning. He begins to walk toward the scent with an air of caution about him. To the right of him hanging on the wall are many beautiful works of art. Some are enormous in size and proportion. One in particular, *The Mona Lisa,* make him stop. Most individuals know of this famous oil painting. Being an avid collector of books, John was entranced by the sight of this beauty.

On his entranceway table at home, he has an art book with this painting in it. Always too sheepish to actually purchase a real piece of art, he finds comfort in viewing them from the pages of the books. Here, now to see it in its true form, a period from long ago, is truly incredible. He inches his way up to the painting. He reads the plaque next to it and stretches his head up to look onto its beauty and great detail.

"This is better than the bowl of waxed fruit I have at home," chuckles John to himself.

At that moment, he swears the painting smiles at him. There has been much controversy surrounding this magnificent piece of art in modern day. One, in particular, was whether or not the painting depicted Leonardo DaVinci disguised as a woman. As long as Leonardo was happy in the life he lived, then so be it. Many art critics felt he painted himself into the portrait to show his desire to be a woman. It was all speculation, and unless you can speak directly with the artist, you will never know. However, taking into consideration the evening's events, that may not be so impossible at this point.

Realizing he was not there to critique art, John turns away from the wall heading down the beckoning corridor. He finds marble stairs that seem to wind up and around and disappear behind a huge stone wall. This leads to the main chambers of the Pope. John knows it is there, and he must fight and perhaps never return. As he is about to take his first step up, he stops. He listens for any signs of life. He listens for any voices from beyond but here's nothing. He senses he is all alone and can hear his own heart beating.

Proceeding up, he moves like a snake in the grass. Every twist and turn must be maneuvered cautiously and without making a sound.

"Lord, if you can hear me, hear my prayer.

Guide and protect me from our enemy. Amen."

As he reaches the top of the stairs, the walls begin sway back and forth. It is as if they have become elastic. They are being manipulated by unseen hands. This now makes it hard for John to have balance and move ahead. He stumbles onto a red carpet and feels dizzy. Under his breath he speaks.

"It knows I am close. It won't let me in. I must try harder to clear my thoughts." Pulling himself up, he grips onto the moving walls. He is clutching on for dear life. He grows pale.

Five

At John's home, the four souls gather for a vigil and sit praying for his safe return back.

"I can't stand not knowing. This is what makes John and I such great business partners. I need to know it all, yesterday, and he gets all that I need today," smiles Heinrich.

The group is puzzled by his comment but is too tired to care at this point.

"Cousin, you must stay positive and focused for John. The past is behind us now. It is the future he fights for. How did this ever happen?" asks Lauren.

Peter begins to interject about his dream he told John back at his home. He explains that

John was chosen by the hHand of God to lead the way to salvation—not to have a judgment day until it is our scheduled time to pass—at which point, it is believed we all get judged with a movie reel of our past. We are then placed into the appropriate realms to continue our learning and help other living souls. Or, we are condemned to our sins and are placed in the lower dwellings to relive our terrible ways of life over and over again, until we can hear the angels calling us to change our ways.

"This is all very interesting and perhaps I believe some of what you are saying. However, how does this help John?" questions Heinrich.

Peter responds sadly, "It doesn't."

He goes on. "If it is his fate to live or die by the hands of the good or evil then so be it."

Everyone grows silent and prays even harder. The consequences are surreal, and John is facing them. Each soul goes over in their minds all the good and bad things they have done in their own lives, somehow trying to reverse it in case it is their time, a reflective moment. They do not know that aside from them, John and those left in Rome they were the only good souls left roaming the earth. The planet has become lifeless. Thirty-three minutes remain until judgment day.

At the end of this enormous grand hall lies the room in which the ritual has begun. As John has the doors in his sights, the hall begins to narrow and stretch out like a rubber band. Again, this is a second attempt to prevent his arrival.

Meanwhile, inside the chambers the high priest has begun to speak. A growling noise is heard throughout the Vatican. It echoes and vibrates off every square inch. Yet, John cannot hear. The priests look up from their Bibles, and search with their eyes around the room to see where the noise could have come from. A Cardinal stands up while two priests try pulling him back down for fear of the uncertainty of their survival. He clutches against his chest a trembling bible.

"Who is there? Is it you we command? Is it you that creates the havoc upon mankind? If it is, I command you to release all the souls you have entrapped back to the Kingdom of God," instructs the high priest.

Nothing is heard. Confident that it was probably just a noise, he sits back down and resumes his reading. The other priests are petrified but cannot allow this to be known. Out of the darkness, lunges a green heavy fog like cloud that forms an arm with nails reaching outward. The priests look up and sees the formation grab hold of the Cardinal's throat. It pulls him up three feet above the floor, dangling him as if he were a piece of meat. One of the priests musters enough strength to speak.

"It's choking him. Quick, grab the Bible and throw it into the circle," he shouts, but it's too late.

The Pope rises from his chair, now feeble and weakened, aged a hundred years over. He stretches his neck and speaks. "I command you back demon. It is I you seek. Let him go!"

The arm releases the limp high priest collapsing to the floor with a horrid thunderous sound. The other two priests rush to his side but it is too late. There is no breath of life in him anymore, but his soul has gone to God for the demon did not take it. The arm turns toward the Pope and begins to form again. This time, it is now erected as a nine-foot tall mass of evil. It appears as half-dragon and half-dog. It has seven horns and seven hooves. It snarls and drips saliva from its mouth. It stares hungrily into the dying eyes of the Pope.

"You have come to finish your deed with me, have you not? asks the Pope.

"Indeed, I have and will complete the task at hand," responds the demon.

Its tail whips back and forth smashing everything in its path.

"I hate everything you stand for and your meager little world you live in is now nothing but a black core of hate," proudly snickers the demon.

Outside the room, poor John is now blind.

His weak body can take very little at this point. He crawls on all fours and is able to pull up to the doorknob. He knows he must get into that room or everything was for nothing. He prays.

"Glidiana, Gabriel, Jesus, please give me one more ounce of your strength to open this door. I, in turn, relinquish my soul to the Kingdom of God in lieu of the ending of this magnificent world." John slides off the door and collapses in front of the chamber. He is unconscious.

Six

"And he said to me, 'These words are trustworthy and true. And the Lord, the God of the spirits of the prophets, has sent his angel to show his servants what must soon take place. And behold, I am coming soon.'"

John's body is lifted in a ball of light and flipped over. He awakens stronger than ever and speaks as he turns toward the doors and flings them open to bang against the walls.

"I, John, am he who heard and saw things. And when I heard and saw them, I fell down to worship at the feet of the angel who showed them to me; but he said to me, 'You must not do that! I am a fellow servant with you and your brethren the prophets, and with those who keep the words of this Book. Worship God.'"

The beast howls in pain as it quickly turns to face John, who is floating in mid-air at the level of his enemy.

"You dare fight me? Do you know who I am? You will be an added bonus to my collection when I shall hang your disheveled soul amongst all the souls I have taken from your sad and pathetic world," shouts the beast.

"John, NOW!" cries out one of the priests on the floor.

How he knows his name and that he was the one was irrelevant at this point. John summons the great chain off the shores of Seattle and commands it to come here. On the beach the chain digs its way to the surface of the sand and flies up in the air and toward the direction of Rome. The beast grows angrier and impatient.

"I have wasted enough of my time with you. You are mine now to take. Where is your God now, I ask you? Where is your Jesus?" sarcastically asks the beast.

"Who do you think holds me up? Do you think a human being can float and glow? I am already dead. You are barking up the wrong tree," says John.

The beast is confused. It should sense this but it has been tricked itself.

"I am God and I am Jesus. I am everything good and strong," says John.

With that, a huge sound is heard above the ceiling, and it begins to fall apart. Above the beast the great chain comes crashing down. It lands around the circle and awaits its master's command.

"No, this cannot be. You will not entrap me. I am Satan. The ruler of the underworld and I am millions of tortured souls against your puny God. You cannot have me. No man can ever rid the world of evil. I am always here, waiting and watching," says the beast.

John cannot remember where the key is. He tries to stall the beast as it begins to stomp its gnarly feet toward him. John swiftly moves about the room side to side, trying to escape the beast. It swings at him, trying to smash him to the ground. John fears the beast will step on the chain and break it. He tries to get the beast away from the chain.

John has to think quickly as every second counts as they're fighting for all their lives and for humanity. As beads of sweat pour down John's forehead, dripping down the side of his neck, he looks over to one of the wall hangings in the room. Then he quickly looks back at the chain struggling to hold onto it. He is only a couple of feet away from the wall behind him where there are two large hooks. He has moments to figure out how to get them as it may be their only saving grace.

As he glances at the wall behind him, one of the priests takes notice trembling in fear, figures out what John is thinking. Suddenly, the priest decides to start shouting passages from the Bible at the beast to get its attention. It works. As the beast makes a loud grunting and snorting sound, it wields its entire body towards the priest in the back of the room. John sees his chance and grabs the hooks out of the wall.

What the beast did not know is that these were not ordinary wall hangings for tapestries but rather a very rare and precious metal said to be a found in the tomb of Jesus of Nazareth. These artifacts were taken and created into pieces that are used in the Vatican for prosperity for hope and faith. It also didn't hurt that it was dipped in holy water!

The beast grows wary of the priest as its tail flings around, and it snaps the priest up coiled like a snake, then releases the lifeless body back into the room. John grabs the hooks and jabs them into the back side of the tail of the beast. It causes great agony as a shrill screeching sound pierces the edges of the room. Everyone covers their ears except the lifeless priest, of course.

"It will be fun to beat you this way. We shall

have a real fight, you and I," says the beast.

Its eyes yellow with hate and malice oozes from its every pore. It gets hold of John by his foot and swings him out the Vatican windows onto the streets of Rome. John is dazed but he gets up. He realizes he is no longer within the walls of the room and needs to get back in there to finish the ritual. Out comes the beast flapping its dragon wings and thundering down onto the ground in front of John. It is ready to do battle. John closes his eyes and floats up. Dawn is fast approaching and Jesus is just above him. He opens his eyes and sees a figure from the distance. It is the great King, his hair flowing with his robe. He looks on at the street as if to wait for the end. The beast gives out a yelping screech as it senses Jesus. There is little time before all that is — will be no more. Only a handful of souls will remain in the entire world, but these very important souls would be the key for new life.

If John can fulfill his destiny, there will be a grand day coming.

At John's home, everyone feels the earth tremble when the beast touched ground. The earth shakes as if you could feel the two doing battle from around the world. Heinrich believes that John was in the moment of fighting the beast.

"It is happening. Let us go outside to pray in the open skies," says Heinrich.

They all decide to go out and pray to the angels and to God to help John in his fight. Peter turns to Heinrich and looks a bit frightened.

"What it is?" asks Heinrich.

"I see John. He is not himself. He is trying to get the beast in the circle. I fear he will not make it. I fear we are all doomed," says Peter.

Heinrich does not know what to say to that. He is upset and doesn't want the others to hear. He tries to stay positive and focused as Lauren has reminded him to be.

"Don't worry, my friend," Heinrich says as he places his hand on his shoulder. John knows what to do. He has been waiting his whole life for this moment. It is God's will. Now, let us pray."

In Rome, Jesus looks on to the battle. John demands that the beast release the souls he has stolen.

"You are to give back those you have forsaken to the Kingdom! If you don't, I will send you back to that pit you call home," cries out John.

"Ha! Nonsense. Do you really think I would just hand them over?" says the sly beast.

"Yes, I do," says John. "What happened to you, Satan? You were one of the most beautiful of beautiful angels." You didn't have to get greedy. You can still have it all but without malice. God would have given you eternal happiness and free reign over those you could teach. Why not begin now, and let those poor souls go? You don't need them anyway. They're all pure of heart and wouldn't be much good to you. You know this."

The beast grows silent. Astonished at what John is saying, it doesn't understand the tone of the words. For centuries, the only things to be said to Satan were the words of being cast out and turned away. No one has ever used kindness in dealing with it. It is trying to digest what has been said to it.

"You speak of a time that is no more. I am not interested in beauty as you can see. I can be anything I want. If I choose to be beautiful, I would. I choose not! Why do you speak to me this way when you know I am going to take your precious world?" asks the beast.

"I know you can release those souls to me, and I speak to you as such," says John.

The beast grows impatient and angry. "Enough of this babble. You try to trick me with your kind words, but that is an emotion I do not understand. It died when I did. And now, you shall die," says the beast.

It runs toward John snarling, its arms out to grab him. John rises up above the beast and flies around him to the other side. It has become a game of tag.

"It seems you have missed some souls on

your list, my friend," says John.

The beast slows down and responds.

"I have not! What is this you speak of!" demands the beast.

"I speak of all the souls who went into hiding around the world from you. They are still alive and breathing waiting for this to end. You have not done your duty, I am happy to say."

What John speaks of is not true, but he tries somehow to discourage the demon from thinking that it is. Angered by what John speaks, the beast begins to question itself. At that moment, John seizes the opportunity to fly under and around the back of the beast and shove its rear back up through the broken window of the Pope's chambers. Down it goes, falling through the floor. Its legs are hanging down below and its wings are caught above its body in the Pope's room. The Pope gets up and speaks to the demon.

"You will not win this battle. John is the chosen one, and he has the strength of many. Give back the souls now or you will be banished to hell forever!" yells the Pope.

"I will not be defeated, old man," snarls the demon.

He swings one of his wings back and then forth and hits the Pope in such a way that he falls down to his knees. John comes flying into the window and sees what is happening. He flies down to the Pope and grabs him around his waist. He lifts him up and out of the window onto the street below. There he rests the Pope's head under his sweater and tells him to relax. He will be okay.

The Pope looks up and says, "God bless you my son, you have done well. Our Lord is proud to have a soul such as yours." With that, the Pope passes out.

Seven

"He who testifies to these things says, 'Surely, I am coming soon.' Amen. Come, Lord Jesus!" belts out one of the priests in the room, still croucheing behind a table.

The beast turns its head toward the priest and laughs sinisterly.

"You call upon your savior, do you? Well, let me tell you about your God. He is not real. He is many that claim to be the answer to your salvation. All your God wants is your soul. So, I say why not give it to me. What is the difference? Your species are such easy prey either way. You all lose in the end. Whether your God or I get your soul, you will still be soulless. Go ahead and give your soul to him. You are a fool. Come with me willingly and I shall grant you a second life. One you can't imagine. You can have anything you desire and still roam the earth if you choose. I will preserve your human body so that you may continue on. So, I say to you, priest, give me your soul and I shall give you eternity."

The priest, mesmerized by the beast, steps forward. He sits down in front of it and stares.

"Good. Now, come a little closer and all shall be yours," the beast breathes heavily.

"No, don't do it. Get away from him. Father, get away now, he is tricking you for your soul!" belts out John, who comes flying back into the room toward the priest.

Seeing John, the beast quickly breathes fire onto the priest and tries to burn him alive. John grabs hold of the priest and brings him downstairs to the holy water. There, he douses him until he awakens. He is badly burnt but he will survive. He lays the priest on the floor and turns to go back. Suddenly, the Vatican begins to shake. The beast is working its way free. Then it goes quiet.

"Help me, someone help me, please," cries out a woman's voice. John turns around and heads toward the voice. A beautiful fair-haired woman is on the floor looking to have been injured. She looks up at John.

"I didn't know anyone was here. Do you know what is going on? What's your name?" John asks.

"I was taking a tour here and the next thing I know, the lights went out and the city grew dark. Everyone was screaming and people just vanished around me. I have been hiding here until I heard voices and felt safe to come out. My name is Natasha."

John is thrilled to see another human being.

"I thought everyone good had been eradicated. Are you hurt anywhere?

"No, no, I am fine. Thank you. Well, I guess we should try to leave this place," says Natasha.

John explains to her there's nowhere to go. He further explains that he must leave her because he has some business to attend to, and she should not be in the building.

"I can stay with you," she offers.

She grabs his arm and when she sees his face she lets go and excuses herself. She doesn't know her own strength sometimes. John begins to sense he should go upstairs and finish the beast before it's too late. He looks over at the priest lying on the floor and decides to go check him before going. As he approaches the priest, the priest trembles and looks past John.

"What is it, Father? Do you want to say something?" asks John.

The priest is shaking his hands. He lifts one of his arms up halfway to try and point to something past John. His eyes are wide and look of fright. Then, his arm falls down to the cold, hard marble floor and is silent. John gets an eerie sensation, and he stands up slowly. All of a sudden, a slithering forked tongue comes sliding right underneath his legs. He turns around and out of Natasha's mouth is the tongue of evil. She is laughing heinously. Her eyes are cold and black. Her hair grows snakes all over. John goes over in his mind what could have gone wrong. How could he not realized this would happen?

"Ah, come on now, you must admit that is a pretty good trick. Don't be a sore loser, John. I can give you eternal life if you come willingly. This whole thing can be over," hisses Natasha.

"What is your name!" commands John.

No reply. The woman just stares at him, her tongue flickering about hissing.

"What is your name, woman!" commands John again.

"I'll give you a hint being you're such a good sport. Drop the ha and you have me."

John says to himself the word Natas. That doesn't make sense. Natas. Then he flips it around—Satan.

"So now you're no longer a beast but a woman?" asks John.

"It was getting a bit cramped in this building. Besides, I wouldn't want to ruin any more of your kind's precious artwork," says Satan.

"You are a card. You really should rethink your position. All you have to do is relinquish the souls you stole to me and, in turn, I will not chain you to the pit," says John.

"Mmmm, tempting but I will have to pass. You will not be chaining me to anything, my dear boy, but I must say I am rather enjoying this conversation we are having."

"I am glad you enjoy anything. That shows me you are capable of doing as I have asked," says John.

Angered by his response, Satan raises her arms and screams at the top of her rotted lungs. Now in a deeper voice she shouts at John.

"I am done with you, mortal. You are to die now, here in your holy of holy places," Satan says and stomps about.

John backs up, knowing this is it. He prays one last time for guidance and strength. He lifts up and dives toward the woman. He grabs her by her neck and starts choking her. He summons the great chain from upstairs, which comes flying down the stairs to the entrance of the Vatican. He tells it to encircle them and lock in place. Satan is howling and grunting and panting furiously. John summons the key that comes from his pants pocket and slides into the lock in the great chain. Satan's eyes watch the key fly around it. Its forked tongue tries to grab it in mid-air. It gets a hold of the key. It begins to laugh as John tightens his grips around the neck.

"You should have stayed a dragon and a dog my friend. This is too easy."

John summons the key to lock the great chain. Just then, Satan's tongue starts burning as the key drips holy water. The tongue drops the key and it slides into the lock. It clicks in place. John releases the woman's neck and flies back out of the circle.

"I command you to the depths of your bottomless pit you call home. You are to release all the souls you have taken this very day and give them back to the Kingdom of God. You must pray for forgiveness, fallen angel. May God be with you," ends John.

Satan is cursing in Latin and speaking backward. He is spitting at John and screaming in pain. All his tricks have failed. The floor beneath the Vatican begins to crumble as if an earthquake is beginning. Pieces of the Vatican begin to fall apart. John has to get out of there. Satan is returned back down into the ground far away from earth.

John collapses to the ground and passes out.

The Vatican stops falling apart. There are some who survived the beast and they emerge from out of hiding. The sun rises over the horizon.

The world slowly heals as it is safe again to go outside. Citizens try to keep other citizens from doing any more harm. It is going to be a long haul but order needs to return. Some fragments of the government remain. Some heads of state come together to devise a plan for all the countries affected by the terror they have just endured.

Many presidents are alive so they begin relief

efforts globally. It doesn't matter who needs help. There is no color, race or creed. Everyone is equal and everyone needs the same thing.

Back at John's home, Heinrich, Eli, Lauren and Peter gather by the shoreline near John's house and watch the sunrise.

"I wonder if John will get a ride back home from Gabriel. I mean, do you think any of the airlines are operating right now?" says Heinrich.

"Oh, Heinrich, you're too much. I think we just have to wait and see. Meanwhile, I suggest we all go back to our homes and take a nice hot shower and eat something. Then let's all do a phone call chain in case John returns," suggests Eli.

Peter is silent. Lauren nods tiredly in agreement. They get into John's car and one-by-one, go home.

Several hours pass and the TV news stations are up and running on a few local channels. Apparently, there had not been a lot of good souls in TV, at least none worth taking. So, many are left to continue on with their daily routines around the world. Word is out about the Vatican being the worst place hit. The Pope has been hospitalized but is expected to make a full recovery. The priest in the entrance way had a heart attack but the doctors are hopeful he will survive with a lot of care and watching. He keeps muttering the same words over and over again: "It's the devil, it's the devil ..."

A cleanup crew is underway and slowly tries to get the Vatican up and running in time for the Pope's return. There's so much confusion everywhere you turn, but in every city and town most of the souls that were spared have had a change of heart. They seem to be helping others in a time of crisis. This is, indeed, a good act and a good thing. Although many will still act out in their bad ways, many will also stop their habits. Many will turn over a new leaf and try and find better things in their life to be happy about. It won't be everyone, but more souls than before may enter the Kingdom one day. And so, the day started with a sense of newness and fresh beginnings. Many have been lost and many have been found. Amen.

Eight

Night falls quickly and the world seems to be at peace since the previous twenty-four hours. The phone rings at Peter's house. It's Heinrich just checking to see if he is alright. He is the oldest out of the bunch and this has taken a toll on his health. He has been coughing a bit.

"Thank you, Peter, I can see why John chose you for a friend," says Heinrich.

"I think that was John's plan all along, but he just didn't know it," says Peter.

"What plan is that?" asks Heinrich.

"Well, I believe the four of us are now connected through this horrible experience. I think we will all be wonderful friends and extended family" explains Peter.

Heinrich becomes a bit choked up with emotion and clears his throat.

"Yes, well, that would be nice. I really am worried about John. Shouldn't he have been back by now?" asks Heinrich.

"Yes, I know what you mean. I have already checked in with the others and they feel it, too. Where is he?" says Peter.

"Well, let's talk in an hour or so and see where we're at," suggests Heinrich and they hang up the phone.

The night comes and goes and there's no sign of John. All who remain soul-wise at the Vatican are the two priests, the Pope and some of his council members. There are their eyewitness accounts of John, but no one knows where he has gone.

The next morning, the four get together over breakfast. They meet at Heinrich's home in town. It's a bright, sunny, clear day. The air smells as if it has been cleaned with scented fabric softener. As Lauren sips her tea, the men go about their conversation over the events and how different they feel toward life in general. They all wanted to be better at their lives and do more good works.

There is a bit of a rumbling heard up high. Down on Earth, people assume it is the remaining storm from the night before. Actually, it is the welcoming of all the souls who were being returned to the Kingdom. Souls were flying left and right, top and bottom, their faces happy and free. At the head of the line are the greeting angels who explain everything to the lost souls. Many are confused and want to go back. It is a hard time for the Kingdom and very busy. There are so many to deal with. Extra angels are on call this day. Family and friends of the past come forth to aid as well.

This is a transition time for those who perished without being ready. As each new soul is greeted at the gate, life on earth is getting back to what is the "new" normal.

* * *

The chit chatter rings in John's ears as he slowly awakens. He feels a bit groggy but okay. Underneath him lay hundreds of white feathers. As he slowly sits up, his eyes try to focus on where he is. All he can see is white around him. Then he hears the sounds of a babbling brook.

Soon in the distance a small cross over bridge forms along with a huge garden of every flower imaginable. He recognizes some, being a lover of flowers. He got that trait from his mother. He stands up on the feathers and stretches out a bit. He feels great. He doesn't remember feeling this good in a long time. Always working and not sleeping on the right mattress, he could afford the newest styles but he refused to switch due to his ability to cope. He was comfortable enough not to be bothered with change. The sun shines and there aren't any clouds in the sky. He walks around and sees if he can find someone. Then, he notices on the bridge are two people approaching him. When they come into view he cannot believe his eyes. It is his mother and father. They all run to each other and gather in a group hug.

"Am I dreaming? Mother, you haven't aged and you, Father, look at your trim waist!" exclaims John.

"Son, you look great to us. We're so glad to be with you again," his father says.

"We didn't want to overwhelm you this being your first day and all. There are many others for you to meet," says his mother as she points in the direction of the garden.

"Go there for a walk and see who else is there for you. We will wait here by the bridge," says his mother.

John hesitantly goes as his mother tells him to. He is just so thrilled to see them. He has been through so much that this is a real treat. He walks over to the bridge to see who else would be there. He thinks he's being thrown a welcome home party. Suddenly, he sees a man who seems very familiar to him. This man turns around and faces John. He wears a long cloth-like robe and his eyes are wide and kind.

"Hello, John. Welcome. You have done well

and your world will continue on as planned. Thank you for your bravery and selflessness," says the man.

"Thank you. I really would like to see my friends and get back home. Don't get me wrong. I just know they are worried sick over me," explains John.

"I see," says the man. "Well, John, I will tell what I will do for you. You can go visit them for a while but you're really needed here now. Besides, your family is here, and it would be nice for you to stay and help us."

John is a bit confused but thinks it over.

"Okay, then. I do want to be with my family, but I will miss my friends, too. Well, when can I see them?" asks John.

Back at Heinrich's house it is very early the next morning. He is still sleeping in his bed. A bright light appears in front of him with a silhouette of a person. It's John.

"Heinrich, wake up. Heinrich, it's me, John. Wake up. I've come for a visit."

Heinrich tosses and turns for a moment and

then falls back asleep. He thinks he is dreaming. John goes over to his friend and talks closer in his ear.

"Heinrich, wake up. It's John."

Heinrich's eyes open and he sees his friend's face. He quickly sits up.

"My God, it's you. You're okay? What happened? What took you so long?" Heinrich rambled on.

John hushes him and told him that he hadn't much time.

"I am sorry, my friend, but I cannot stay. I am allowed to come and say a few words but then I must go," he explains.

"Please run the business however you see fit. Give my share to one of your children's foundations. Give my home to a family called Johnson who cannot afford one. It is already paid in full. As for my personal belongings, give them to the poor and take whatever you would like. I won't be needing anything anymore like that. I will miss your face but I promise I will pop in from time to time. I must go. Tell the others the same and that I love you all."

John backs away into his light and disappears in the room. Heinrich rubs his eyes a hundred times in disbelief and is not comprehending what just happened. He doesn't know what to do. He wants to know where John is. He thinks he'll be back later on. He rests his head on the pillow and falls asleep again.

John visits the rest of the group, but they are all sleeping. He smiles at each one of them and gives them a blessing. When they wake up they will feel new and more alive than ever before. They will go on to lead better lives and do more for people they know and don't know.

The world slowly works its way back to being civilized. There was much work to be done but his four friends will be instrumental in the process. They will go on to do great things. John returns home to see his parents. There they are waiting for him.

"Did you have a nice visit son?" asks his father.

"Yes Dad, I did. I will miss seeing everyone

and will miss my work," says John.

"Yes, that is hard, but there is a new job for you. Let's go over the bridge and get you started," says his father.

As they are walking, John thinks about his time in the Vatican. He reminisces over the art he witnessed. Suddenly, he has a feeling that there iss a presence behind him. He stops walking and turns around. A man with a heavy Italian accent begins to speak.

"Oh my, you're that artist!" John exclaims.

"Yes, well, I still do that, but I also do many, many more exciting things. Come, I will show you," says Leonardo DaVinci.

"Hey, I have to ask about that painting. Your *Mona Lisa*? What is it really about?" John asks eagerly.

"My good fellow, it is about everything and nothing. Walk with me and your parents, and I will reveal to you," says DaVinci.

"Also, what about these codes that people went on about?" asks John.

"Ah, never mind all that. Let them create

what they want down there, and I will continue to create what I want up here. Now, we must go!" orders DaVinci in his thick, Italian accent.

The four of them cross over the bridge and into the field of endless flowers. It has no borders. Everything just keeps going as far as the eye can see. John is getting ready for his new job. But first, a party is thrown in his honor. All the great artists and writers are going to attend. Also, family dating back for centuries will be there waiting to meet their relative from the modern world. What a grand day it is up high! What a difficult one it will be down below.

- The End…Or Is It? -

About the Author

Alexandra Holzer has appeared in numerous film documentaries exploring the paranormal, on TV as a paranormal expert, and as a guest or guest-host of hundreds of national talk radio shows. She also created a paranormal segment for Reading Pennsylvania's morning show WY102 on WRFM, a commercial FM radio station. As a result of her ongoing contributions to the field of the paranormal, Holzer has been featured in *Broadly-Vice Magazine, Rolling Stone, Rue-Morgue, Fortean Times, MTV News Online, The Associated Press,* People.com and *Teen Vogue.* She has also been profiled on Hamptons.com. Holzer is the author of *Lady Ambrosia: Secret Past Revealed* (2007) and *Growing Up Haunted: A Ghostly Memoir* (2008). Holzer's other written works include: contributions to AOL's *Huffington Post,* Canada's *UFO Digest,* and the popular, holistic, green-zine *OM Times,* and is currently a contributing writer to the UK's print and online *Haunted* magazine.

A well-respected East Coast-based paranormal investigator, "sensitive," journalist and author, Alexandra is inarguably living the life she was born to live. Her father was the late author, lyricist, lecturer, educator, spiritualist, and parapsychologist — Professor Dr. Hans Holzer, PhD, who is known all over the world as the original Ghost Hunter, with over 150 published titles, non-fiction/fiction, to his name. Alexandra contributed to the creation of the TV series *The Holzer*

Files for Travel Channel (2019-21), making its debut on the 10-year anniversary of her father's passing and diving into some of Dr. Hans Holzer's case files.

Alexandra is the co-founder of the global organization "Hunt with Holzer", a research and investigative organization carrying on *The Holzer Method*, which she and her husband created. Living in New York, Holzer is a tireless mother of six children, ranging in age from 4 to 22, is an advocate for adopting rescue pets from shelters, is a believer in setting wellness goals, and would love to see a cure for childhood diabetes in her lifetime.

Discover more about Alexandra Holzer at alexandraholzer.com

For more information visit:
www.hauntedroadmedia.com

www.ingramcontent.com/pod-product-compliance
Lightning Source LLC
Chambersburg PA
CBHW060336310726

48976CB00007B/2582